AR Quiz #45302
BL 3.7   3pts

ANIMAL EMERGENCY

PONY IN TROUBLE

Other Books in the
ANIMAL EMERGENCY *Series by*
Emily Costello

Coming Soon

ANIMAL EMERGENCY

PONY IN TROUBLE

EMILY COSTELLO

ILLUSTRATED BY LARRY DAY

AVON BOOKS
An Imprint of HarperCollinsPublishers

For Jared Samuel Dalone

1

"Hey, Stella! Come meet my new kitten!"

Nine-year-old Stella Sullivan looked toward the gas station. One of the attendants was waving at her. He was wearing a tan coverall with his name sewn above the pocket and a baseball cap.

"Who's that?" Stella's friend Josie Russell whispered. The girls were on their way to Stella's house. It was Saturday and Josie was going to spend the night. They were hurrying because it was cold outside.

"Bud," Stella said. "He has a ferret named Freddy. Freddy is one of Anya's patients."

Anya was Stella's aunt, and the only veterinarian in their small town of Gateway, Montana. Stella wanted to be a veterinarian, too, when she grew up. She spent as much time as possible at Anya's animal clinic. By watching Anya work and helping out when she could, Stella was learning a lot about animals.

Stella and Josie ran over to where Bud was standing near the garage. Inside, two other men in overalls were working on a shiny red truck that was up on a lift. Seeing the dull underside of the truck reminded Stella of looking at an X ray.

A tiny kitten was twisting around Bud's feet. She squeezed her eyes half closed and rubbed her face against his ankles. Stella could hear her deep-throated purr.

"She's beautiful," Stella whispered. "What's her name?"

"Jane," Bud said.

Bud reached down and scooped the kitten up in one hand. Jane was black with a white nose, ears, and boots. Bud held her against his chest. Jane clung to him with fine, chalk-white claws.

"When did you get her?" Stella asked.

"Last week," Bud said proudly. "She's a naughty girl. Keeps me up at night, pouncing on my eyelashes while I'm sleeping. Eats like a pig. Yesterday she even got into my boss's lunch box."

Stella giggled. "Can I hold her?"

"Sure." Bud pulled the kitten away from his chest.

"Mrrrr," Jane protested, clinging to Bud.

Bud gently unhooked her tiny claws from his coverall.

"Don't be scared," Stella whispered as she cuddled the kitten against her chest. Jane sank her claws into Stella's jacket.

Josie yawned, impatiently shifting her weight. She watched the mechanics, pretending not to be interested in the kitten. Josie was a ranch kid, and she was always saying Stella was too emotional about animals.

Stella fought the desire to roll her eyes. Why did Josie have to pretend not to like kittens? *Everyone* liked kittens. Even tough ranch kids like Josie.

"Rrrruf! Rrrruf!"

A dog was barking. Somewhere very close by.

"Ow," Stella said.

Jane had really sunk her claws in now. She was panicked—trying to climb over Stella's shoulder. Her miniature back legs were surprisingly strong. Stella felt the sharp points of Jane's claws against her skin. She reached up and struggled to grab the kitten.

Bud was also reaching out toward Jane. Josie looked around, trying to spot the dog.

Stella saw him first. A sheepdog. He was in the flatbed of a dusty yellow pickup truck that had just pulled into the station.

"Rufrufrufrufruf!" the sheepdog continued.

Stella managed to grab Jane around her belly and pull her off her shoulder.

"Heeeeeeee," Jane hissed. The hair on her back stood up like a Halloween cat's, and her little tail was poofed out like a brush.

"Give her to me," Bud said.

The yellow truck slowed near one of the pumps. The dog leaped over the side and landed a few yards away from them.

"Grab him!" Stella shouted.

Josie moved forward.

Beeeep!

A blaring car horn made Josie jump back.

The dog galloped toward them.

Stella saw a blue car. A little one. A lady with gray hair sat behind the wheel. She was wearing glasses and gripping the wheel tightly.

Squeeeaak came the sound of the lady's brakes. Then—

Thud.

The little car hit the sheepdog and stopped. Stella saw the lady inside rest her head against the steering wheel. She looked like she was crying.

Stella felt as if someone were squeezing her heart in a fist. She drew in a shaky breath.

The dog staggered out from under the little car. He took a few woozy steps and collapsed.

Stella handed Jane to Bud and ran for the dog. "I'll get Anya!" Josie said.

The animal clinic was just two blocks away. Anya would be there in a few minutes—if she wasn't out on a call. Until Anya arrived, Stella was on her own.

"I'll be right back," Bud said. "Just let me put Jane in the office."

Stella fell to her knees beside the dog. His head was down on the oily pavement, his tongue hanging loose. He was unconscious.

But that wasn't the worst part.

The worst part was his leg.

Stella could see it out of the corner of her eye. Raw and red. She shuddered. But Stella couldn't help the dog if she was too scared to look at his injuries. She took a deep breath, screwed up her courage, and forced herself to turn her head. She drew her breath in sharply. Tears sprang to her eyes.

The fur on the dog's leg was slick and dark with blood. Flesh the color of uncooked hamburger showed through where the fur had been scraped off. Stella saw something white and splintery sticking out. She stared numbly for a minute before realizing the white stuff was the dog's bone.

People had gathered around behind Stella. She glanced over her shoulder. Bud. The other men from the garage. The lady who had hit the dog with her car. And another man who had on a filthy canvas jacket and heavy work boots.

The woman had one hand over her mouth. Her nose was running and she was crying. "We—we've got to get him to a veterinarian," she said. She put her hand on the man's jacket. "Oh, oh—I'm so sorry. How can you ever forgive me?"

That man must be the dog's owner, Stella thought. He shook his head and turned away, heading back toward his dirty truck, which was still parked near the pump. Stella felt sorry for him.

And angry. Why had he let his dog ride in the flatbed? That was very irresponsible.

The woman's eyes met Stella's.

"We shouldn't move him," Stella said firmly. "My aunt is a veterinarian, and she's on her way." *I hope,* Stella added to herself.

Stella felt something wet on her knee. The dog's blood had soaked through a patch of her jeans.

"We've got to stop his bleeding," Stella told Bud. "I need a clean cloth."

Bud nodded and ran toward the garage. He was back in a minute, carrying a handful of T-shirts he must have gotten out of his locker. "Here," he said, kneeling down next to Stella.

Stella took one of the shirts and, screwing up

her courage, pressed it into the wound. She could feel warm blood seeping through.

Gross, Stella thought, but she kept her hand in place. If the dog lost too much blood he would die before Anya even got there.

The lady from the car knelt beside Stella. "Thank you, thank you. I'm glad *someone* knows what to do," she said.

That made Stella feel a little better.

Still, she was glad to see Josie running back into the station with Anya just behind her. Anya was carrying one of her medical bags—the one with stuff for small animals.

The lady from the car scurried out of the way, and Anya took her place beside Stella. "Nice compression," Anya said to Stella. "Can you hold it?"

"Sure," Stella said. She felt much braver now that Anya was there. Helping Anya wasn't so difficult. It was making decisions that was hard work.

Anya put her hand on the dog's knee to check his pulse. She looked at his gums and listened to his heart. She was quiet and businesslike as she examined the dog.

"I'm going to put on a tourniquet," Anya announced. She pulled a length of rubber out of her bag and began fitting it around the dog's leg. "Then we'll have to move him so I can operate on his leg."

"Don't bother," came a man's voice from behind them.

Stella turned.

The dog's owner was standing behind Anya. He was pointing a battered shotgun at the dog's head. "I don't have no use for a three-legged sheepdog," he said in a matter-of-fact voice. "I'm going to put Chewy out of his misery now."

"Wait!" Anya said. "Put the gun down and talk to me for a moment." She got to her feet and stood between the man and his dog.

Josie and Bud stood together a few feet away. The lady from the little car started weeping again.

Stella kept her hand on the pressure dressing. Her fingers were starting to go numb, but she knew she had to control the dog's bleeding. Anya hadn't had time to finish putting on the tourniquet.

"Ain't nothing to talk about," the owner said sullenly. "You won't save that leg."

"Let me try," Anya said. "Good sheepdogs are hard to find."

"Well, that's true," the owner admitted. "But I'd

rather spend my money buying a new one than paying a veterinarian for surgery that ain't going to work."

Stella felt a cold fury inside her chest. How could Chewy's owner worry about money at a time like this? His dog needed help!

Anya frowned. "Tell you what," she said stiffly. "I'll do the surgery, and I'll only charge you if I can save the leg."

The owner considered for a moment and then nodded. "Sounds like a good deal," he said, lowering the gun.

"It is," Anya told him.

Stella felt her shoulders relax, and she gave Anya a proud smile. *Anya* understood what was important. Stella watched as Anya swiftly tied the tourniquet and moved Chewy onto a piece of canvas she got out of her bag.

"Will you help me carry him down to the clinic?" Anya asked the owner.

"Sure thing." Now that he was getting no-risk veterinary care, the owner was cheerful. Stella didn't think he should be so happy when his dog was unconscious and bleeding.

Bud was leading the lady from the car into the service station office. He had one hand protectively on her back.

Anya and the owner each lifted two corners of

the canvas. They started down the street, carrying the limp dog.

Stella and Josie hurried after them.

Nobody said much on the way down the street. Stella guessed Anya didn't like Chewy's owner any more than she did.

Anya and the owner carried Chewy up the clinic steps and through the waiting room. Mrs. Crouse was sitting there with her cat, Maggie, in a carrier. Mrs. Orne, Stella and Josie's teacher, was waiting with her ferrets in their carrier.

"Hello, Mrs. Orne," Stella and Josie chorused automatically.

"Hello, girls."

"Oh, dear!" Mrs. Crouse said when she spotted the dog. "Is he going to be okay?"

"Yes," Anya called as she disappeared down the hallway. "But I'll need to reschedule my afternoon appointments. Stella, could you?"

"Sure!" Stella said. She went around to the back side of the reception desk. Anya had a big appointment book there. Josie came around, too, and sat in the swivel chair.

Mrs. Crouse walked up to the desk.

Stella studied the book. Anya was having office hours on Wednesday the next week, but all of those times were full.

"Can you come back on Friday at two-thirty?" Stella asked Mrs. Crouse.

"Sure," Mrs. Crouse said. "I'm just down the street."

Stella wrote "Maggie Crouse" in the slot for 2:30. Chewy's owner came out of the operating room and left while Stella was waiting for Mrs. Orne to step up to the counter.

Mrs. Orne smiled awkwardly at Stella. Stella felt funny seeing Mrs. Orne on Saturday. She felt almost as if she'd been caught playing hooky.

"Can you come back on Friday?" Stella asked politely.

Mrs. Orne consulted a slim date book she had pulled out of her purse. "Yes," she said. "Four o'clock would be convenient for me."

Stella bit her lip and looked at Anya's book. The four o'clock spot was open. Stella hesitated, tapping the book with Anya's stubby pencil. Josie was watching her curiously, as if she could guess what Stella was thinking.

Mrs. Orne was never very nice to Stella. She expected her students to be on time every day, and she never let Stella explain why she was late—even though she often had a very good excuse.

Stella considered telling Mrs. Orne she had to come at a different time. Or on a different day.

No, Stella decided. She didn't know why Dultercup and Violet needed to see Anya. It could be something serious. The ferrets shouldn't suffer just because she didn't like Mrs. Orne.

"Four is great," Stella said. She wrote "Buttercup and Violet Orne" in the empty spot and gave her teacher a virtuous smile.

After Mrs. Crouse and Mrs. Orne left, Stella locked the clinic door. Then she went to the door of the operating room to see what was happening.

Anya was dressed in scrubs with a cap over her hair and a mask on her mouth. Chewy was on the operating table. The overhead light shone down on him.

"Can Josie and I do anything to help?"

Usually, Stella would have joined her aunt in the operating room. But Josie couldn't stand the sight of blood and Stella didn't want to leave Josie alone.

Anya looked up for a split second before focusing back on Chewy. "Yes. Could you cancel the rest of my afternoon appointments?" she asked.

"Sure," Stella agreed. She went back to the reception desk and looked at the book. Three more people were scheduled to come in. Stella called each one and changed their appointments.

Then she opened the door of Anya's office. Rufus, Stella's puppy, bounded out.

"Rufrufrufruf!" he greeted her, twisting himself in a tight circle.

"Hi, boy!" Stella picked Rufus up. She gave him a hug and a kiss.

"Let's go for a walk!" Stella snapped a leash on Rufus. He ran to the back door and stood waiting.

"You, too, Boris," Josie said. "Come on, boy!"

Stella patted her thighs. Slowly, Anya's big basset hound emerged from under Anya's desk. He gave Stella a baleful look as she snapped on his leash.

Stella took Boris and Josie took Rufus. Once they got outside, Rufus ran ahead and then back. They weren't walking fast enough for him. He reminded Stella of herself during recess back when she was a kindergartner.

Boris plodded along on his short bowed legs, letting Stella know he preferred to spend the afternoon on his pillow under Anya's desk.

Stella's mind was with Anya in the operating room. She crossed her fingers and hoped Anya would be able to save Chewy's leg. What would happen to Chewy if she couldn't?

Back at the clinic, Stella and Josie did chores they knew would help Anya. They fed the animals in the boarder room—two elderly German shepherds. They answered the phone.

Still, Anya didn't come out of the operating room.

Josie and Stella sat down in the boarder room

and played checkers. Stella didn't want to go home until she knew Chewy was out of danger. Her parents wouldn't worry as long as she and Josie were home by dinnertime.

Stella sat up straighter when she heard Anya step out of the operating room. Anya had pulled off her green surgical gown and cap. But Stella could see a line on her aunt's forehead where the cap had squeezed.

"Is he okay?" Stella asked.

Anya sighed. She looked tired. "Well, yes and no. I couldn't save his leg. But he should do just fine. There's no reason Chewy can't have a happy and useful life with three legs. Dogs adjust very quickly."

Stella's heart sank. Anya was trying to put a brave face on it, but Stella knew her aunt was disappointed.

"What will his owner say?" Josie asked.

"We'll have to wait and see," Anya said quietly.

Stella was worried as she and Josie and Rufus headed home. The owner didn't seem like the kind of man who would change his mind easily.

The next morning was cold and crisp with a beautiful, brilliantly blue sky. Stella felt hopeful as she and Josie set out toward town with Rufus on a leash.

Sunday and sunny. Nothing bad could happen on such a nice day. Chewy's owner would change his mind about not wanting a three-legged dog. Stella was sure of it.

Rufus trotted proudly along at Stella's side.

"He likes his coat," Josie said with a laugh. Norma, Stella's mom, had just bought the little dog a bright red coat that snapped under his belly. Little dogs weren't good at keeping themselves warm.

"He knows he looks handsome," Stella said.

They followed a path into the woods. This was the fastest way into town, much faster than following the roads. Stella and Josie liked it because it gave them a chance to keep an eye on their favorite skating pond. So far the pond had only a few spiky pieces of ice near the edges. Stella couldn't wait for the pond to freeze over.

After passing the pond, they crossed into an open field covered with two inches of crusty snow. Stella felt Rufus stop and stare across the field. She put out a hand to stop Josie.

"What do you see, boy?" Stella whispered. She stared into the white field.

There! A flash of movement.

Rufus lowered his upper body and let out a low growl.

"I think that's a badger," Josie whispered.

The animal was twenty yards away. The badger was tan with a blocky body. He had a small pointed face with a mask—-kind of like a tan-and-brown raccoon.

He stared toward Rufus and the girls while nervously continuing to dig in the half-frozen ground. He'd already turned up a mound of fresh brown dirt that stood out against the white snow.

"What's he doing?" Josie wondered.

Stella stood still and watched. The badger was watching them uneasily, as if he knew he should run away but didn't want to.

"Come on, boy," Stella said after a long moment. She took another step forward. That was too much for the badger. He fled into the woods.

A moment later, Stella and Josie paused to look down the hole the badger had dug. Stella was astonished to see a small tan squirrel lying in the crumbly dirt.

He wasn't moving.

• **3** •

Stella stood staring down at the squirrel, unsure what to do. His eyes were closed. He looked dead, but there wasn't any blood on his soft brown fur. The squirrel seemed perfectly intact—right down to his adorable little hands, which were clasped together under his chin.

"Did the badger kill him somehow?" Stella asked.

Josie shrugged.

Rufus smiled up at her, his tiny pink tongue hanging out of one side of his mouth.

I'll ask Mom when I get home, Stella decided.

Stella's mother was a wildlife biologist in Goldenrock, the national park that surrounded their small town. She knew all about animal behavior. Chances were she would know why a badger would kill a squirrel and try to bury him.

"Come on, boy, let's go," Stella said.

Stella was about to turn away when a slight movement caught her eye. She stared at the squirrel intently, holding her breath.

After what seemed like an impossibly long time, Stella saw the squirrel's side gently rise and fall.

"Did you see that?" Stella whispered.

"What?" Josie asked.

"Just watch."

One, one-thousand, two, one-thousand, Stella counted silently to herself while keeping her eyes on the squirrel. She got all the way up to *twenty, one-thousand* before the squirrel breathed again.

"He's alive!" Josie said.

Watching the squirrel's slow breaths had made Stella aware of her own breathing. She inhaled and exhaled at least four times as frequently as the squirrel did.

"He's hardly breathing," Stella said. "We have to get him to Anya."

Moving swiftly now, Stella took off her jacket and sweater. She still had on a T-shirt, but it wasn't much protection against the cold morning air. She quickly pulled her jacket back on and zipped it up.

Kneeling down next to the hole, Stella picked

up the squirrel. Before, he had seemed almost like a stuffed animal, a toy. Now that Stella held him in her bare hands, she could see he was real. She didn't feel any warmth from his body and this made her hurry even more.

Stella wrapped the squirrel in her sweater and began to run toward the clinic.

Josie ran with her, holding Rufus's leash.

"Ruf!" The puppy thought they were playing a game. He ran happily along at Stella's side, occasionally jumping up against her knee to show how excited he was.

Stella was breathless and sweaty by the time they got to the clinic. She found Anya in her office, working on the computer.

Anya took one look at Stella's face, another look at the sweater in her hands, and jumped to her feet. "What do you have?" she asked.

"A squirrel," Stella gasped. "I saw a badger trying to bury him. He's hardly breathing."

Anya took the squirrel carefully from Stella and rushed into Exam Two, where she gently started to unwrap the sweater.

Stella and Josie trotted after her.

"I know I'm not supposed to handle wild animals," Stella said, "but he's out cold and I knew it would be easy to wrap him up without getting bitten."

Anya had the squirrel exposed now. She gently ran her fingers over its delicate legs and down its tail. From experience, Stella knew Anya was testing for broken bones.

"The badger didn't do any harm," Anya said. "Just dug her up. You must have scared the badger away just in time to stop this little girl from becoming a furry snack."

"Dug her *up*?" Stella asked. "I thought the badger was *burying* her."

"Nope," Anya said. "This is a Uinta ground squirrel. They live in burrows."

"How do you know it's a girl?" Josie asked.

"I got an A in my squirrel anatomy course," Anya told her with a wink.

Stella leaned closer. "If she's not hurt, why doesn't she wake up?"

"Hibernating," Anya explained.

Stella felt silly. Hibernating! She should have thought of that. But she had never actually seen a hibernating animal. They were always hidden away in caves and underground.

"I should have left her where she was," Stella said.

Anya shook her head. "No, she would have died exposed to the weather."

"What are we going to do with her now?" Stella asked.

"We're going to let her wake up, give her a snack, and then take her right back to her burrow. She'll have a better chance at returning to hibernation if she isn't awake for long."

An hour later, Stella and Josie were watching the squirrel frantically nibbling on a peanut. The bottom of her cage was littered with peanut husks.

Anya came in and peeked over their shoulders. "Waking up takes a lot of energy. The food and water we gave her will help her replace the energy she lost. I just hope she hasn't been awake too long."

"What do we have to do?" Josie asked.

"Hustle her out to the field and open the cage," Anya said. "Don't touch her now that she's awake! Squirrel bites can be bad."

The cage had a handle. Josie and Stella each picked up one side. They carried the cage outside and cut into the woods.

Stella wanted to hurry, but they couldn't go fast with the cage. They stumbled along, moving as quickly as possible. The squirrel sat up straight and alert. But she didn't stop nibbling on her peanut.

Ten minutes later, when they got back to the field, Stella's fingers were cramped and aching from carrying the cage.

They put the cage down in the snow. Stella stepped forward, unlatched the door, and swung it open.

The squirrel sniffed the door. She put one paw outside. Then she dashed out and disappeared into the same hole the badger had dug. The girls could hear the squirrel scritching and scratching at the dirt.

Five minutes passed.

Then ten.

No more noises came from the hole.

Stella and Josie cautiously approached. The squirrel was gone, but Stella thought she could see a patch of disturbed ground.

"I think she dug herself back into the burrow," Stella said.

"Cool," Josie said.

Stella nodded, feeling relieved the squirrel was where she belonged. She just hoped the badgers would leave her alone until spring.

The girls locked arms and headed back to the clinic. Josie needed to call her brother, Clem, for a ride home. Stella needed to get Rufus.

On their way through town, they stopped at the drugstore and bought a handful of nickel candies. Stella felt wonderful because the squirrel was going to survive and because her peppermints tasted so good.

"Is that a horse?" Josie asked as they approached the clinic.

The animal was tied to the railing next to the clinic's front steps. He was nudging at the icy snow to get at Anya's scruffy winter-killed grass.

Weird, Stella thought. People never brought their horses to the clinic. They were too big and there was nowhere for Anya to house them. Anya always did house calls for horses.

"No," Josie said, answering her own question. "It's a pony."

"Must be an emergency," Stella said. "But where's Anya?" Without knowing why, Stella started to run. Something strange was going on at the clinic. Anya didn't just leave ponies tied to her railing.

"He's sick," Josie said as they got closer.

Stella could see that, too.

The pony's hipbones and ribs were clearly visible under his coat. He looked as if he hadn't had a good brushing in months. His brown-and-white hair was dull and matted with dirt. His hooves were messy, and he was holding one off the ground as if it hurt him.

Josie got to the pony first. She stood a few feet away, staring in disbelief. Stella stopped next to her.

The pony didn't look up to greet them. He didn't

stop his nudging at the ice. His expression was dazed, distant—as if he had completely given up.

"Poor sad thing," Josie whispered. She moved closer to the pony and wrapped one arm around his neck. With her other hand, she rubbed his muzzle.

The pony rested his head against Josie's shoulder and let out a sad sigh.

"Y-you'd better get Anya quick," Josie said.

Stella paused. Was Josie crying? She could hardly believe it. Then she shook herself and ran up the stairs two at a time.

• 4 •

"**A**nya!" Stella yelled.

No answer.

"Anya!" Stella wondered what was happening in the clinic. Anya hadn't even noticed there was a pony tied to her railing.

Stella stepped into Exam One and then Exam Two. Both rooms were empty. Next she tried Anya's office. Her aunt was sitting in her swivel chair with the phone tucked between her shoulder and ear. She was frowning and scribbling on a notepad as she listened.

"Chewy is recovering nicely," Anya said. "I took him for a walk today and he—"

She's talking to Chewy's owner, Stella realized. She crossed her fingers and prayed he would change his mind about not wanting a three-legged dog.

"I see," Anya said shortly. "Well, thank you for your time." She hung up the phone a bit more forcefully than necessary.

"What did he say?" Stella asked, although she was pretty sure she knew.

"He said to put him to sleep," Anya said.

Stella felt as if someone had dumped a load of bricks on her chest. "What are you going to do?" she whispered.

Anya stood up and tossed her pen onto the desk. "I don't know," she said.

Stella didn't like that answer. Was Anya saying she might put Chewy to sleep? That was so unfair! Chewy was a perfectly healthy dog. So what if he was missing a leg? And besides, that wasn't even his fault. If his owner had kept him in the cab of his truck, Chewy never could have jumped out and gotten hit.

"I'll ask Mom and Dad if I can keep him," Stella said. "They might—"

"No," Anya interrupted. "Chewy is a working dog, not a pet. He needs to be on a ranch where he can run all day."

Stella didn't know how to argue with that. Besides, hearing the word *ranch* made her remember Josie waiting outside.

"There's a pony tied to the railing," Stella reported.

Anya looked surprised. She grabbed her horse bag and headed straight outside. "Oh," Anya breathed as she came down the steps. "Poor pony!"

Josie hadn't moved from the pony's side. "He's hungry," she said. "Can we feed him?"

Anya gave her a businesslike nod. "I have some hay in the back shed. Bring a bucket of water, too."

Josie headed for the backyard. Stella ran inside and found a bucket in the boarder room. She filled it with water and carefully carried it outside. Josie came around the building with her arms filled with hay.

As soon as Stella put down the water, the pony stuck his muzzle in. Stella could see his throat working as he drank.

"That's enough," Anya said. "You'd better take that away before he makes himself sick."

Stella glanced at her aunt. Anya's voice was tight, her face flushed. Stella was surprised. She'd seen her aunt in all sorts of difficult and dangerous situations, but she hadn't often seen Anya so angry.

"What's wrong with him?" Stella asked as she grabbed the bucket and gently pulled it away

from the pony. He turned immediately to the hay Josie had piled at his feet.

"He's been neglected," Anya said, running her hand gently over the pony's ribs.

The pony ignored her. He was chewing mechanically on a mouthful of hay.

"Probably for weeks," Anya said bitterly. "Who could do this?"

"Is he sick?" Josie asked quietly.

"Malnourished," Anya said. "He needs food and water, grooming, his hooves trimmed and reshoed." She kept circling the animal, studying him—as if she couldn't believe what she was seeing.

"But he's essentially sound?" Josie asked.

"A poor diet can lead to all sorts of complications," Anya said. "Brittle bones. Infections . . ."

A family—a man and a woman with two little boys—stared at the pony as they passed in front of the clinic on the sidewalk. Stella watched them for a moment, wondering if they were going to come forward and claim the pony. But they just kept walking.

"Don't worry," Josie told the pony in a low voice. "We're going to take care of you now."

"What happened to his owner?" Stella asked.

"I looked for a note while you were inside," Josie said. "But I didn't find anything."

"I doubt we'll see the owner again," Anya said. "What am I going to do with him?"

"We can't leave him outside all night," Josie said. "He's already shivering. Once the sun goes down it's going to be way too cold."

"True," Anya said. "He needs a cozy place in a barn."

For a moment, they all stood staring hopelessly at the pony. Stella didn't have any room at her house for a pony. Josie shifted her weight from foot to foot, biting her lip.

"Maybe we could board him somewhere," Stella suggested doubtfully. "Um—do you think Jake would help?"

Jake owned a stable where Stella's sister, Cora, worked.

"He's still rebuilding from the fire," Anya said. Jake's barn had burned down the previous August.

"Oh," Stella said. "Right."

"We have a little extra room in our barn," Josie said decisively. "I'm going to ask my dad if we can take him in temporarily. He's not contagious or anything, is he?"

"I'll give him a thorough workup and make sure," Anya said. "Some vitamins wouldn't hurt, either."

Stella stared at Josie in disbelief. Her best

friend was always telling her she was too soft. Josie made fun of Stella for trying to save every sick or injured animal in Gateway. What had gotten into her best friend?

Josie marched into the clinic to call her dad on his cell phone.

Anya went to work examining the pony. "Don't get your hopes up," she told Stella. "Josie may want to help the pony, but she still has to convince her dad."

Stella nodded. She'd already thought of that. Josie's father was one of the hardest people Stella had ever met. *He'll never let Josie take in the pony,* Stella told herself. Mr. Russell wouldn't want to waste the feed, and he wouldn't want Josie to waste her time on such a sad creature.

But when Josie came down the clinic's back stairs, she had a triumphant grin on her face. "Clem is bringing the horse trailer," she announced. "Daddy said the pony can stay for a whole week."

"That's great!" Stella exclaimed.

At the same time, she braced herself for an unpleasant experience. Clem Russell was the closest thing Stella had to an enemy. Josie was unsentimental, Mr. Russell was hard and businesslike, but Clem was just downright mean. He and Stella had battled frequently.

Still, Stella kept her opinions to herself. Josie was fiercely loyal to her family. Stella knew how upset she'd get if Stella said anything bad about Clem.

Half an hour later, Clem pulled up in front of the clinic in his beat-up Ford pickup. He had the Russells' brown horse trailer hitched up behind.

Clem hopped out of the truck and came striding up the clinic steps. He dressed like a younger version of his father: cowboy hat, neat denim shirt, clean jeans held up with a belt sporting a huge silver buckle, and the best cowboy boots money could buy. Over that he had a corduroy jacket lined with lambswool.

"Anya," Clem said in greeting. Clem had to be polite to Anya. She was an important person—the local veterinarian. He ignored Stella and Josie completely.

Clem circled the pony and let out a low whistle. "This here critter is more dead than alive."

Stella felt her spine tense up. Clem was going to make fun of the sickly pony.

"A few square meals will change that," Anya said. "I examined him and he's essentially sound."

Josie smiled.

Clem shook his head. "I'd like to get hold of whoever did this," he said angrily. "Maybe see how he likes going without proper food and water."

Stella was surprised for the second time that afternoon. Never in her wildest dreams had she expected Clem to be sympathetic toward the pony.

She watched as Clem carefully positioned the trailer so the pony wouldn't have to walk too far on his painfully overgrown hooves.

Josie used a handful of hay to lure the pony into the trailer.

"You coming?" Josie asked Stella after the pony was safely loaded.

Stella looked at Anya. "Do you mind dog-sitting Rufus?"

"No problem," Anya said.

Stella gave her aunt a grateful smile and climbed into Clem's pickup for the trip back to the ranch. As soon as they got there, Clem parked the pickup near the barn and went back to his chores.

Josie carefully unloaded the pony and led him into the barn. Her sleek black colt, Gus, watched as Josie led the pony into the clean and empty stall next to his.

Stella filled the water trough and Josie shoveled in some best-quality hay. The pony immediately began to feed.

Josie went into the tack room and came back with two soft brushes. "Be careful around his bones," she warned Stella. "If you brush too hard you'll injure his skin."

Stella fit the brush over her hand and went to work. Josie did the same. Cleaning the dirt off the pony's hair and smoothing out the knots was deeply satisfying. The girls worked quietly for a long time.

"I'm going to call him Everest," Josie said thoughtfully as she ran her brush over the pony's hip.

Stella didn't say anything right away. Hanging out at the clinic had taught Stella the importance of giving an animal a name. Naming an animal made it something you could love. "Why Everest?" Stella asked.

"Because his bones stick out like mountains," Josie explained.

Stella nodded without speaking. She wondered how Josie would feel when the week was up and they had to find another home for Everest.

• 5 •

onday was cold with a steely gray sky. Stella hurried through town after school, eager to get to the clinic and get warm.

I've got to talk to Anya about Chewy, Stella thought as she scurried down the sidewalk. She couldn't let Anya put the dog to sleep. Somehow she had to find a way to save him. If it hadn't been for Everest, she would have asked the Russells to take him in. But now that seemed like a long shot.

As she approached the clinic, Stella could see Anya standing outside. She wasn't wearing a coat—just her usual jeans and work shirt. She had her arms wrapped around her chest for warmth.

Anya was talking to a man Stella didn't recognize. He was wearing a gray cowboy hat with a broken rim. He stood crooked—as if his back hurt. His huge belly strained against the tattered flannel shirt he wore under an equally tattered jacket.

Stella stopped next to Anya. She could tell from her aunt's pinched expression that Anya was mad.

"I want him back," the man said furiously.

"Fine." Anya's voice was calm but cold. "But first I'd like to know why you dumped him on my steps."

"Let me tell you something, lady," the man said nastily. "James T. Harden"—with this the man poked his chest with one dirty finger—"does not just leave his assets lying around."

Stella moved closer to Anya. She'd figured out the man was Everest's owner. She felt like stomping on his toes. He'd practically starved the pony to death. And now he was telling Anya what to do?

"Then how did the pony get here?" Stella demanded. Her face was starting to feel hot.

Anya glanced at Stella. Her expression was hard to read, but somehow Stella got the idea Anya wished she weren't there. Well, too bad. Stella wasn't going to leave Anya to face Mr. Harden alone.

"Joel!" Mr. Harden spat out the name. "Never should'a hired him. Stupid bleeding heart. And a thief! He stole my property."

"He stole your pony?" Anya asked.

"Stupid bleeding heart," Mr. Harden repeated. "Nobody else ever complained. Ponies have a limited useful life. We always sell them the same week we shut down the farm for the winter. Just makes good business sense. Feed ain't free, you know."

"Well, from the looks of him you didn't waste much feed on that pony," Anya said.

"He was supposed to be auctioned off yesterday!" Mr. Harden shouted. "Now I'm going to have to make an extra trip just for this bugger. You think gas is free? Three hours at the auction. I ought to charge Joel for my time. That would teach him! Young people today have no appreciation for the value of a dollar."

"That's not true!" Stella said, burning with fury.

Mr. Harden ignored her. "Listen, I don't have all day to argue with you," he told Anya. "Just let me know where to find my pony and I'll be on my way."

Stella stared up at Anya. Her aunt's eyes were narrowed, her lips tight. She hated Mr. Harden as much as Stella did.

Anya won't tell him where Everest is, Stella thought. *She wouldn't.*

"Wait here," Anya ordered Mr. Harden. She turned around and went into the clinic.

Mr. Harden stomped his feet and scowled at Stella. Stella trotted after Anya, leaving Mr. Harden alone in the cold.

"What are you going to do?" Stella demanded as she followed Anya into her office.

"Ruf! Rufrufruf!" Rufus ran out from under the desk and jumped up against Stella's calves, begging her to pick him up.

"Call Assistant Sheriff Rose," Anya said.

Stella bent down to scoop up the puppy. "Shhh, boy," she said. Rufus panted and wiggled with joy. "You're going to get Mr. Harden arrested?" Stella asked Anya. "That's a good idea. After what he did to Everest, he deserves—"

Anya smiled sadly. She shook her head as she dialed the phone. "I wish I could put him away," she said regretfully. "But actually I—"

She held up one finger and then spoke into the phone. "Hello! This is Anya Goodwin. May I speak to Rose please? Sure. Thanks."

Stella could see that her aunt was waiting for Rose to come to the phone. "But treating a pony that way must be against the law," she argued quickly. "And if it's not, it should be. How would Mr. Harden—"

Anya gestured for Stella to be quiet. "Rose, got a little situation here," she said into the phone. "Yesterday Josie and Stella found a pony on the clinic steps. He was in pretty rough shape—still is, actually. The owner just showed up and demanded him back."

Stella shifted her weight impatiently as Anya listened to Rose. She couldn't believe it—but it actually sounded as if Anya was considering giving Everest back.

Unbelievable! Sometimes Stella just didn't understand adults.

Stella thought of Josie. Everest had been all she could talk about that day at school. Josie could hardly wait to get home and check on him. Clem was going to help her trim his hooves that afternoon. She said the pony was already gaining weight. And he had made friends with Gus, her colt.

"You're sure?" Anya said into the phone. "Okay. Yes, I understand." She replaced the receiver slowly.

"What's happening?" Stella asked warily.

"We have to give the pony back to Mr. Harden," Anya said.

"We can't!" Stella shouted. "Josie loves him— Mr. Harden doesn't. He doesn't even feed him. You saw how hungry the pony was."

Anya sighed and rubbed her hand over her eyes. "Rose says we have no choice. Come on," she said wearily. "Let's get this over with."

"No," Stella said stubbornly. She crossed her

arms in front of her chest. "I won't help him get Everest back."

"I understand," Anya said softly. She moved around Stella and went back outside.

Still holding Rufus, Stella rushed to the window in the waiting room. The window looked out on the front steps. From there, Stella could see Anya talking with Mr. Harden. She rubbed her cheek over Rufus's fur while she watched Mr. Harden pull a notepad out of his pocket and make a few notes. Then he turned, strode down the steps, and climbed into a pickup truck. The whole conversation didn't take more than two minutes.

Anya came back inside.

"What's happening?" Stella demanded.

"Mr. Harden is going to get his horse trailer," Anya said.

"You mean he's going to Josie's right now?" Stella asked.

Anya nodded sadly. "The auction is tomorrow."

Auction? Stella felt her anger subside a bit. "He's going to sell Everest tomorrow?" she asked.

"Yes," Anya said.

"Well, then, that's not so bad," Stella said. "Whoever buys him will definitely treat him better than Mr. Harden does."

Anya glanced down at the floor. "Maybe," she said. "We can hope."

Stella studied her aunt. There was something she wasn't telling her. Something bad. "What's wrong?" Stella asked.

Anya let out all of her breath at once and looked up to meet Stella's gaze. She seemed to make a decision. "The auctions," Anya said. "Usually there are some people there from the slaughterhouses."

"So?" Stella asked. "They'd be after cattle and goats—not Everest. Not ponies."

"It's an equine auction," Anya said with a little shake of her head. "Horses and ponies only."

Stella stared at her aunt, refusing to believe what Anya was telling her. Why would slaughterhouses buy ponies? People wouldn't eat the meat.

Anya saw Stella's confusion. "The meat is shipped to other countries," she explained. "Mostly in Europe."

"People in Europe eat pony meat?" Stella asked. Anya nodded.

Stella felt her stomach churn. An image of Everest's sad dark eyes filled her head. She was imagining him marching up a chute to his death—

No! She couldn't let that happen.

Not to Everest.

Not to Josie.

She was going to stop Mr. Harden somehow.

Stella put down Rufus. "I've got to call Josie," she announced.

"Sure," Anya said.

Stella rushed into the office and dialed the phone. She waited while it rang and rang. Maybe Josie wasn't home yet. Or, if she was home, she was out in the barn with Everest and Gus.

"I've got to go over there," Stella told herself as she put the phone down. Then she grabbed her jacket and quietly let herself out the clinic's back door. She didn't want to see Anya. She didn't want to give her aunt a chance to stop her.

As Stella ran through town, she longed for her bike. The Russells' ranch was a twenty-minute bike ride outside Gateway. It would take Stella much longer on foot.

Stella didn't know how long it would take Mr. Harden to get back to wherever he kept his horse trailer, hitch it up, and drive out to the Russells'. But she wanted to get there before he did. She wanted to have plenty of time to talk to Josie, to come up with some sort of plan.

By the time she reached the outskirts of town, Stella's lungs were burning. Her legs felt heavy. She was sweaty inside her winter jacket.

She slowed down and walked.

We've got to save Everest, Stella told herself as

she plodded through the brittle snow on the side of the road. Maybe if she got to the Russells' ranch in time, they could hide Everest somewhere. Or . . . drive him out onto the Russells' pastureland. Mr. Harden would never find the pony on the Russells' vast ranch.

Stella was getting cold. She started to run again, half to warm up, half out of her eagerness to get to Josie's.

She ran. Walked. Ran some more.

Compared to the roads in town and the ones leading into the park, this one was practically deserted. Only two or three vehicles passed Stella. Nobody she knew.

Finally, Stella turned into the Russells' drive. She hoped Josie wouldn't be out in the pastures somewhere. If she was, it could be hours before she came back. Then, Stella would have to deal with Mr. Harden on her own.

Stella opened the back door of the house. "Josie!"

The kitchen was messy. A handful of new eggs sat on the counter, feathers still clinging to them. The garbage can was overflowing.

Most days, Josie, Clem, and their father rushed in and out of the house, doing only what they had to do to keep the place halfway clean. The house wasn't where they lived. They lived in the barn and out on the land. Things were different when Josie's mom was alive. Then the house had been cozy and welcoming.

Stella ran out toward the barn. The building was like the rest of the Russell ranch—functional but not fancy. The barn walls were made of cement block, the floors were concrete, and the stalls had sliding metal doors.

"Josie!"

Josie stuck her upper body out of Everest's stall. "Hey, Stella! Come see Everest! You're not going to recognize him."

Stella hurried down the aisle and stopped outside of the stall. Everest looked like a different animal. He was still thin—but his coat was gleaming and his hooves were now neatly trimmed and reshoed.

The pony nudged Stella with his muzzle, and she saw that his eyes had lost their dull, dead look.

Josie was still working on him, rubbing oil into his hooves to make them shine. "How did you get here?" Josie asked, sounding pleased by the unexpected visit. "Can you stay for dinner?"

"I ran," Stella said.

Josie glanced up from her work and noticed the look on Stella's face. Her smile faded. "What's wrong?" she asked.

"Everest's owner is on his way here," Stella said. "He's going to take Everest and sell him to a slaughterhouse." She was prepared to explain how the meat was shipped abroad, but Josie already seemed to know about this. Anyway, she didn't ask any questions.

Josie slumped forward as she took in the awful news. She sat staring at the straw under Everest's hooves, her arms hanging loose between her legs. "I can't believe Everest is going to die," she said heavily.

Stella felt like shaking Josie. "He's *not*," she insisted. "We're going to save him."

Josie laughed bitterly and shook her head. "How?"

"We can drive him out into the pasture," Stella said forcefully. "When Mr. Harden gets here, we'll tell him Everest got away somehow. Then, maybe tomorrow, we could move him to Marisa's."

Marisa Capra was one of the girls' classmates. Her parents ran a bed-and-breakfast—a kind of small hotel—and kept a few animals for their guests' amusement.

"Dad and Clem won't be in for another hour," Josie said thoughtfully. "I guess it won't hurt to try."

"That's the spirit!" Stella said.

Josie jumped to her feet and pulled a horse blanket off a nail. "Everest doesn't have much meat to keep him warm. Let's wrap him up. And he's too weak to ride. We'll have to go get him as soon as Mr. Harden leaves. I don't want to leave him out all night."

"Hurry," Stella said. "Mr. Harden could be here any moment."

"Help me." Josie tossed the blanket over the pony's back. Stella bent down to fasten it. Josie grabbed Everest's halter and quickly tightened the straps.

Everest sensed their tension. He twisted his head to watch their hurried movements and shivered nervously under Josie's touch.

"Let's go, let's go," Stella said.

"We need a horse," Josie said. "Can you saddle up Honey?"

"Sure," Stella said. She ran down the aisle to the tack room and grabbed the first saddle and saddle blanket she saw. She rushed back to Honey's stall and slipped the blanket over the mare's back. Stella threw on the saddle and fastened the buckles as quickly as she could. Her fingers were stiff with cold.

Josie led Everest down the aisle. "Let's go."

"I'm almost there," Stella said. She fastened the

last buckle. The girls quickly led Everest and Honey out of the barn.

They'd only taken two steps into the yard when Stella saw Mr. Harden's black truck turn into the drive. He waved as he drove toward them.

"What should we do?" Stella said.

"Nothing," Josie said limply. "It's too late."

She was right. Mr. Harden was pulling up, right next to Josie. They couldn't hide Everest after Mr. Harden had already seen him.

"Let's not waste time," Mr. Harden said as he hopped out of his truck. He pointed at Josie. "You—take your blanket off my pony. The halter is mine. I'll take that."

Mr. Harden moved around Everest, and quickly began pulling off the blanket.

"Stop!" Josie said, pushing his hands away.

Mr. Harden stepped back as if she had slapped him. "Girl—is your mother home?" he said harshly. Clearly he didn't like being ordered around by a child.

"No," Josie said defiantly. "My mother . . . isn't home. Or my father."

This information seemed to make Mr. Harden stand taller. "Well, I'm sure they won't mind if I take my own property. I don't have all afternoon to wait for them to get here, you know."

"Keep the blanket," Josie said. "I don't want Everest getting sick."

"Everest? Who is that?" Mr. Harden demanded.

"The pony," Stella told him.

Mr. Harden shook his head in disgust. "What kind of person names other people's ponies?" he muttered to himself. "What a waste of time."

Stella noticed that Mr. Harden didn't argue with Josie about the blanket. Instead he moved around to the back of the trailer and threw the doors open.

"Naaawww!" Everest backed away from the trailer and neighed. Mr. Harden swooped forward and snatched up the pony's lead rope. He pulled. Everest locked his legs and leaned back.

"Bloody bugger!" Mr. Harden cursed. "I don't have all day to fight with you."

Stella had a sudden thought. "Mr. Harden, we want to buy Everest," she said. "That way you won't have to waste your time at the auction."

Mr. Harden stopped and squinted shrewdly at her. "How much money do you have?"

"Um . . . none right now," Stella said. "But Josie's father is going to give her the money when he gets back. If you just leave Everest here, you can have the money tomorrow."

Josie's eyes widened in confusion. Then it dawned on her. A beat too late, she nodded enthusiastically. "Oh, yeah, my dad is very interested in this pony."

Mr. Harden dismissed them. "Have him call me. Until then, I'm taking my property. I didn't ride all the way out here for nothing."

"Let me give you some hay," Josie pleaded. "For Everest to eat tonight."

Mr. Harden gave no sign he heard her. He began to jerk on the rope again. The force pulled Everest's head forward. The pony leaned back.

Stella clenched her fists and squeezed her eyes shut. She couldn't bear to watch Everest struggle. She wanted to make Mr. Harden stop but she didn't know how.

"Girl—hold this." Stella opened her eyes and saw that Mr. Harden had dropped the rope. He climbed into the trailer.

Josie stepped forward and picked up the rope. "It's okay," she whispered to Everest. Her voice sounded thick and strangled. "Everything is going to be fine."

Mr. Harden stepped out of the trailer. He was holding a switch. Before Stella or Josie could react, he raised the switch and brought it down on Everest's backside.

Crrack!

"Naw!" Everest jumped in pain. But he still refused to enter the trailer.

"Stop it!" Stella yelled. She ran at Mr. Harden and hit him on his back. With one hand he pushed Stella, knocking her to the ground.

Crrack! Mr. Harden brought the switch down again.

Josie fell to her knees next to Stella. "You okay?"

Breathlessly, Stella nodded. Her eyes were hot with tears. She stared up at Mr. Harden, hating him more than she had ever hated anyone in her life.

Crrack!

"Naawwww!" With the last cruel impact, the fight went out of Everest. He dragged himself slowly up the ramp and into the trailer—almost as if he knew he was on his way to die.

Mr. Harden laughed. "Third time's the charm!" He slammed the trailer doors shut. Then he turned and pointed a finger at Stella. "I can see you take after your busybody aunt. Well, if you know what's good for you, you'll stay out of my way."

"And I'll thank you to get off my property!" Josie hollered, getting to her feet and brushing off her knees.

"With pleasure," Mr. Harden said. He climbed into his truck and started up the motor. The girls watched as the trailer bounced down the driveway. They could hear Everest neighing sadly.

" 'Bye, Everest," Josie whispered as the trailer turned onto the road.

• 7 •

The girls were still talking about what to do when Mr. Russell and Clem rode in from the field. They looked tired and cold. They swung expertly off their horses and led them into the barn.

"I better go get dinner," Josie told Stella. "After we eat, I'm going to ask my dad for the money to buy Everest."

"Good luck." Stella gave Josie an encouraging smile, even though she didn't feel very hopeful.

Josie nodded. "I'll see you at school."

Stella began the long walk back into town. The light was fading out of the sky and the temperature was dropping, but Stella didn't hurry. Her feet felt like lead weights. She couldn't get the sound of

Everest's sad neighing out of her mind. She wondered what was happening to the pony now. He probably wouldn't get any feed or water. *I wish Mr. Harden had taken Josie's hay,* she thought.

It was after five by the time Stella reached town. As she passed the service station, Stella remembered her father had asked her to stop and invite Bud to have Thanksgiving dinner at their house.

Stella didn't feel like stopping. She was tired and hungry. All she wanted to do was get Rufus and go home. But Thanksgiving was only three days away. Her father wouldn't be happy to find out she'd put off asking Bud.

She could see Bud from the sidewalk. He was washing the windows of a lime-green Volkswagen beetle. The owners were leaning against the car, reading a road map.

Stella waved and motioned for Bud to come talk to her when he finished. She wearily wandered into the garage, heading for the drinking fountain.

Bud's kitten, Jane, was crouched down near one of the hoists. The cement floor under her was stained with spots of shiny engine oil.

"Hi, kitty." Stella was surprised to see the kitten loose in the garage. She held out her hand and knelt beside her, cheered by her furry face.

Still hunkered down, her bony shoulders sticking out, Jane looked up at Stella and licked her lips. The kitten had been licking something off the garage floor.

"What are you eating?" Stella asked. She picked up the kitten with one hand. She was so light!

Rufus had taught Stella that puppies will eat almost anything—manure, panties, shoes, even old cold brussels sprouts. Rufus would even eat things that would make him sick. Stella had a feeling Jane was the same way.

"Mrrreeeew," Jane protested, eager to get back to her snack.

"Hang on a second." Stella put a fingertip into the bright puddle. Was it oil? No. Oil was brownish black. Whatever this was, it was bright blue.

"Hi, Stella," Bud said as he came into the garage. "Thanks for catching Jane. I usually keep her in the office, but she got away from me when that car pulled in."

"No problem . . ." Stella hesitated. "Bud, what is this stuff? Jane was licking it." She held out her finger so Bud could see the blue liquid.

"Antifreeze," Bud said. "You know, the stuff that keeps engines from freezing up in the winter."

"What's it doing on the floor?"

Bud shrugged and petted Jane between the ears. "One of the mechanics must have spilled it.

Plenty of people were having it put into their radiators today. Supposed to freeze solid tonight."

Jane was still licking her lips. She didn't look distressed, but Stella had an uneasy feeling. A chemical that stopped your radiator from freezing couldn't be good for kittens to drink.

"Do you have a bottle of this stuff?" Stella asked.

"Boxes of 'em," Bud said. "Why?"

"I just want to check something," Stella said.

Bud shrugged again and headed over to a metal shelf crammed with tools and car parts. Still carrying Jane, Stella followed him.

"My parents want you to come over for Thanksgiving dinner," Stella told Bud. "I mean, if you don't have any other plans."

Bud gave her a slow smile. "That would be nice," he said, sounding pleased. "I don't have any family in Gateway, and Thanksgiving has always been a special favorite of mine."

Now Stella was glad she'd stopped. "We're going to eat at noon," she said as Bud rummaged around on the shelf.

"Tell your mom I'll bring some homemade bread," Bud said.

"Okay," Stella agreed. She smiled to herself, imagining Bud baking bread.

"Here you go." Bud handed her a black bottle of antifreeze.

Stella looked at the label and felt her heart leap. There it was. A skull and crossbones. And, in bold type, a warning: "Severe poison. Keep out of reach of children and pets. In case of accidental ingestion, contact a poison center immediately."

"Bud, we've got to get to the clinic now," Stella said. She was already moving toward the door.

"Why? What? Stella? Kevin—I'm going to take a break. Watch the pump!"

Stella tucked Jane under her coat and started to jog. Was it her imagination or was the kitten starting to act sluggish?

She ran out of the service station and onto the sidewalk. She could hear her heart pounding in her ears.

Bud was right behind her. "Stella—what's going on? Why do we have to go to the clinic? I'm supposed to be working . . ."

Stella ran past The Wooden Spoon, a diner. The parking lot was crowded. "Antifreeze is poison!" Stella called to him.

She kept running. Up the clinic steps. Through the deserted waiting room. "Anya!" she yelled.

"In here!"

Anya's voice was coming from Exam Two. Stella and Bud ran into the room. Anya had Chewy on the table. His backside was covered in bandages

but he was awake and alert. He looked up and sniffed the air curiously.

Stella stared at Anya and Chewy, feeling her throat start to tighten up. Why was Chewy on the table? Could Anya actually be putting him to sleep?

"Anya—what are you doing?" Stella demanded harshly.

"Jane drank antifreeze," Bud announced.

Chewy had gotten a whiff of the kitten. "Ruf!" He barked fiercely, trying to scramble to his feet on the slick stainless table.

"Give Jane to me," Anya said immediately. "Now! Hurry! I've only got a few minutes. Get Chewy out of here."

Stella took the kitten out from under her jacket. Bud had already grabbed Chewy's leash. Anya quickly lifted the dog and put him down, then she snatched the kitten out of Stella's hands.

Bud hesitated. "What's happening? Is she going to be okay?"

Anya looked grim. She plopped Jane into the sink and began throwing open cabinets. "Antifreeze is an extremely fast-acting poison—especially on animals as small as Jane. She probably only weighs a few ounces. We could be dealing with liver damage—"

"Ruf!"

"Get that dog out of here and let me work!" Anya snapped.

Stella took Chewy's leash from Bud and led the dog toward the door, expecting him to stumble and fall. But Chewy seemed perfectly comfortable hobbling along beside her. Stella and Bud withdrew into the waiting room and sank down into side-by-side chairs.

Chewy flopped down at Stella's feet. He stared up at her, panting. Stella stared back. She felt numb. Was Anya really about to put Chewy down?

Rufus was barking. Anya must have had him and Boris locked up in her office. Normally, Stella would have let the puppy out, but all she could think about now was Jane and Chewy.

Bud took off his cap and began twisting it in his hands. "Why didn't I go and get Jane right away?" he asked. "I never should have left her alone in the garage. I knew it was a dangerous place. I should have left her at home where she's safe, but she gets so lonely."

"I think we got her here in time," Stella said.

"Do you really?" Bud asked. He perked up a little, but then slumped down in his seat again. "Anya said a few minutes. A few minutes! How long do you think it took us to get here? Two minutes at least. Maybe three . . ."

Stella wasn't used to being out in the waiting

room. It was awful. She could only guess what was going on back in Exam Two. She kept an eye on the clock over the reception desk. Five minutes passed. Then six. And seven.

What was happening? Anya had said "a few" minutes. By now she should know if Jane was going to live. Why didn't she come out and tell them something?

"If she lives, I'll never take her to the garage again," Bud said fervently.

Eight minutes.

Nine.

Ten.

Finally, Anya came down the hall and into the waiting room. Stella searched her face for some sign. Anya gave them both a weary smile.

"Close call," Anya said.

"She's okay?" Bud demanded. His eyes were wide.

"I'll have to watch her liver function over the next couple of days to make sure everything is working properly." Anya shook her head. "Bud, you sure were lucky this time. If you hadn't come right in, Jane would have died an awful death."

Bud patted Stella on the shoulder. "It was Stella," he said. "She saw the puddle and checked the bottle. She did it."

"Good work," Anya said, giving Stella a wink.

"Thanks," Stella said. Usually, Anya's praise was enough to make her feel wonderful. But not this time. Now she was too worried about Chewy.

"I'd better get back to work," Bud said.

"I've got to get going, too," Anya said. "I'm supposed to be at the White Buffalo Ranch."

"Can I talk to you?" Stella asked quickly.

Anya glanced at her watch. "How about in the morning? I'm already twenty minutes late."

"Okay," Stella said.

"Put Chewy back in his cage for me?" Anya asked. She snagged her jacket off the rack and picked up her keys and cell phone.

"Sure," Stella said. Anya and Bud rushed out, and Stella led Chewy back into the boarder room. She made sure he had more than enough food and water, hoping she wasn't feeding him his last meal.

Stella fell into a deep sleep as soon as she crawled into bed that night. She woke up in the dark with her heart racing.

A nightmare . . .

Stella stared up at the ceiling, remembering images from her dream. Everest walking slowly toward a huge dark building. Anya leaning over Chewy with a syringe in her hand. Chewy's owner pointing his gun.

Outside, the wind was howling. She could feel the cold seeping under the window. Stella shivered as she turned to look at her clock. The numbers glowed in the darkness. 3:17. The middle of the night.

Stella couldn't get back to sleep. She didn't even

want to—not if it meant going back to that dream. She threw off her warm covers and tiptoed downstairs.

Rufus was asleep in the kitchen. He stretched and moaned when Stella picked him up off his pillow. Back upstairs, he curled into a tight ball on Stella's bed and went to sleep again.

Stella pulled the covers up. She rested her hand on Rufus's back. She felt small and frightened for Chewy and Everest, but having Rufus close made her feel a bit stronger. She'd saved Rufus's life. That proved she wasn't completely powerless.

Things seemed better in the morning.

Stella couldn't wait to get to school and find out if Mr. Russell had given Josie the money to buy Everest. She also wanted to get to the clinic in time to talk to Anya about Chewy.

She hurried through her morning routine and rushed outside with Rufus on his leash. Rufus strutted along happily, proud of his red coat.

The sky was a shocking blue. The air was so cold Stella's breath came out in big white puffs. Stella hurried, thinking only of getting to the clinic.

She followed the path into the woods.

"Ruf!" Rufus barked excitedly and rushed forward.

Stella pushed the little button that locked the leash. She didn't want Rufus to get too far ahead. "What is it, boy?" she asked. But by then she had already seen what had gotten Rufus so excited.

"Rufruf!"

"Shh," Stella scolded. "Don't scare them."

A flock of swans was sitting on Stella's skating pond. The birds were big with feathers as white as snow. Their long necks made them look graceful.

"Beautiful," Stella whispered to herself. But at the same time, something about the swans was bothering her. A minute passed before she realized what it was.

The swans weren't swimming.

Swans are usually in constant motion—gliding slowly across the water. But these swans were sitting serenely in place. Occasionally one would flap its wings and then settle them back into place. But they never moved from their spot on the ice.

Ice?

For the first time, Stella noticed that the pond was frozen over. She crouched down and waited. When a swan stretched its wings, she saw that its feet were caught in the ice.

They must have landed on the water last night, Stella told herself. *Then the temperature dropped and the ice formed and caught them.*

How odd!

Stella imagined how she would feel with her feet frozen into ice, unable to move, and her heart started to beat faster. She wouldn't like it. Not at all. She had to do something to help the swans.

But what?

She couldn't go out on the ice and pull them free. The pond had been open water the day before. Stella knew the ice coating the pond now was too thin to support her weight.

Maybe she could throw a rock and shatter the ice. But what if she missed and hit one of the swans?

Stella paced on the ground near the pond, wondering what to do. *Go get Anya,* she decided. She began to rush toward town. A moment later, she and Rufus passed into the field where she had found the squirrel. The dirt the badger had dug up was harder to see now that it had frozen.

Thinking back, Stella was a little embarrassed that she hadn't known the squirrel was hibernating. That thought made her pause and look back toward the pond.

Now, Stella noticed something else about the swans. They didn't seem afraid. They seemed . . . serene. The same way swans always seemed.

Somehow, Stella got the idea the that swans were waiting patiently for something to happen. She glanced at her watch. It was only a quarter to eight. She could hang around for ten or fifteen minutes and still have time to talk to Anya about Chewy before school started at eight-twenty.

Stella went back to the pond. She crouched down next to an aspen tree and settled in to wait. Rufus licked her face. She giggled and let out a few more feet of leash. While Stella kept her eyes on the swans, Rufus happily explored the edge of the pond.

The ice let out eerie creaks and groans. A patch near Stella grew watery as the sun warmed it. Rufus completed his survey and settled in next to Stella.

Stella's thigh muscles began to ache from sitting in one position. But the sun was hitting the back of her jacket and keeping her warm.

Creee-aack!

Stella jumped in surprise as the ice let out a moan. And then—

Fwop! Fwop! Fwop!

A swan quite nearby powerfully flapped its wings and rose up off the pond.

Stella jumped to her feet. Cool! The ice had broken up enough to free the swan.

"Ruf! Rufrufruf!" Rufus scrambled to his feet, startled by the swan's sudden movement.

The swan was only a foot off the ice.

Rufus surged forward, chasing the swan.

"Rufus—no!" Stella said sharply. "Leave the swan alone."

The puppy paid no attention. He raced forward, right onto the ice. "Ruf! Rufrufruf!" He jumped up, snapping at the swan's tail feathers.

The swan rose higher, well out of Rufus's reach. Rufus continued the chase, barking with excitement, his eyes on the fleeing bird.

For half a second, Stella relaxed. The swan was safe. But then she saw the danger. Rufus was way out on the ice. He only weighed six or seven pounds, but still . . .

"Rufus—get back here right now!" Stella yelled.

Rufus stopped and looked her direction. He began to trot toward her.

"Good puppy," Stella said. "Come on!"

Now Rufus was only five or six feet away. Suddenly he seemed to tilt forward. He let out a frightened bark.

Stella gasped. His front paw had gone through the ice!

Rufus scrambled back away from the hole. The puppy began shaking the water off his paw.

"Come on, boy!" Stella yelled impatiently.

But Rufus hated to be wet.

Shake, shake.

The ice under Rufus's rear paws collapsed! He was suddenly half under the water.

Stella covered her mouth in horror. She could hardly breathe as she watched Rufus claw with his front paws, desperately scrambling to get out.

Rufus couldn't get a grip. He slipped. His head went under and disappeared.

For a moment Stella was too surprised and horrified to move. Rufus! She waited, listening to her heart beat, but he didn't come back up.

Stella ran the few steps down to the edge of the pond, scanning the surface of the ice. She had to get Rufus! He'd gone down only a few feet off the shore. Maybe she could reach him. She took a step onto the ice and heard a low creaking.

She looked down. The ice was clear as glass, and Stella could see the water moving and bubbling under her foot. She shifted her weight onto the ice and saw a pattern of cracks spread out around her boot.

Stella jumped back. The ice was too thin to support her.

"What am I going to do?" Stella said out loud. She had to save Rufus somehow. She could imagine him flailing in the cold water, unable to break through the ice above him.

Suddenly, Stella remembered the leash in her hand. She looked down, her mind racing. Would retracting the leash choke Rufus?

Stella was worried—but she didn't really have any choice. She took a steadying breath and then hit the button on the leash's handle.

Btzzz.

The leash slowly began to retract.

Stella kept her eyes on the ice. She could only hope Rufus wouldn't get trapped underneath the ice.

A foot of the leash retracted. Then two. Then—

Stella saw a flash of white under the ice! It was Rufus floating up against the underside of the ice. He was maybe a yard from the hole he'd fallen through. The leash was stretched tight, straining against the edge of the ice.

For a moment, everything held in balance. The leash was as tight as a guitar string. The ice held. Stella's hand shook. If the leash broke she'd have no way of saving Rufus. If the leash broke, he'd drown. Then—

Ping! A sharp sound of something shattering. The ice!

The leash cracked through the ice and began retracting with great force.

Btzzzz . . .

Oh—Rufus! He was sliding toward Stella—half in and half out of the pond. She could see that his eyes were open. He was coughing.

He was alive!

Stella reached way, way out over the bank of the pond. She was crying with relief as she grabbed Rufus's collar and pulled him in to her chest.

Rufus coughed and a great surge of water came out of his mouth. He took a deep rattling breath.

"That's good," Stella told him through her tears. "Get it all out."

Rufus looked miserable. His pretty red coat hung heavily, weighed down by all of the water it had absorbed. His fur was plastered to his skin, and streams of water ran off him.

"Let's get that coat off you." Stella put Rufus down and quickly unsnapped his coat. While she wrung it out, the puppy gave himself a vigorous shake, sending water droplets flying in all directions. Then he sneezed twice.

Stella laughed and brushed the tears off her face. "Feeling better?" she asked.

But Rufus's head was still hanging. The merry look hadn't come back into his eyes.

"What's the matter, boy?" Stella asked.

The little dog shivered and huddled up next to her leg.

"You're cold, aren't you?" Stella said. She unzipped her jacket and put Rufus inside. "Don't worry. I'm going to get you to the clinic right away," she said.

Stella ran down the path, out into the open field, and through town. She could feel Rufus shivering against her. All she could think about was getting him warm.

Anya was coming down the stairs from her apartment when Stella rushed in.

"What happened to Rufus?" Anya asked immediately. She was carrying a cup of coffee in one hand and her work boots in the other.

Stella was gasping for breath. "He chased—a swan onto—the pond and—fell through."

Anya gave Stella an intense look. "You okay?"

Stella nodded quickly. "He's awake and breathing, but I can't get him warm."

Anya reached into Stella's jacket and pulled Rufus out. He was shivering violently, his whole body vibrating uncontrollably. Stella had never seen him look more miserable, not since he was a tiny puppy and half starved.

"He has hypothermia," Anya said.

Stella's eyes widened with concern. "What's that?"

"His core body temperature has dropped," Anya explained. She started back up the stairs to her apartment. "Come on."

"Why is he shaking like that?" Stella asked as she trotted after her aunt.

"That's his body's way of trying to keep warm," Anya said. She walked into the living room. "Shivering speeds up his metabolism."

"What can we do?" Stella asked.

"Help him warm up." Anya stopped in front of her fireplace.

Stella stared. Anya kept a braided rug in front of the fire. Boris, Anya's old hound, loved to lie there. Only Boris wasn't in his usual spot. Chewy was. He lay stretched out with his three feet toward the fire. He raised his head in greeting and then put his head back down. Obviously, Chewy wasn't feeling too well.

Anya rarely brought patients upstairs. Stella wasn't sure what it meant, but she felt a hopeful stirring in her chest. Maybe Anya had decided to adopt Chewy.

"Here, take Rufus," Anya said.

Stella took the puppy and held him close. The shivering hadn't gotten any better.

Orange embers glowed in the bottom of the grate. Anya opened the fire screen and tossed in a few logs. She leaned in and blew. Ashes flew everywhere and the flames licked up around the logs.

"Sit here while I go get some towels," Anya said.

"Okay," Stella agreed. "Thanks, Aunt Anya."

"Don't worry," Anya said. "We'll fix him up."

Stella gave her a weak smile. She could hear Anya rummaging around in a closet and then the sound of the clothes dryer rumbling.

In a few minutes, Anya came back with a bath towel warmed in the dryer. "Wrap this around him," she said.

Stella wrapped Rufus up in the towel. She could still feel his body shivering.

"When that one cools off, we'll replace it with a warm one," Anya explained.

Stella nodded. "Is he going to be okay?"

"Sure," Anya said. "Are you? It sounds as if you had quite a scare."

Stella shuddered. "It was awful. I thought he was going to drown."

Anya smiled at her. "Haven't you noticed? Animals don't die when you're around. Rufus is going to live to be a wise old dog."

Stella's gaze moved to Chewy. He was sleeping peacefully, his side slowly rising and falling as he breathed. "What's going to happen with Chewy?" she asked.

Anya sighed. "I couldn't put him down."

"Are you going to keep him?" Stella asked.

"No," Anya said. "Chewy is a working dog. He'd never be happy as a house pet. He needs to be out with a flock of sheep, doing what he was born to do."

"Even with three legs?" Stella asked.

Anya shrugged. "Why not? Here, let's switch that towel." She got up and came back with a warm towel.

Stella unwrapped the first towel and replaced it with the warm one. She thought she could feel Rufus's muscles relaxing. "I think he's warming up," she said.

"Good," Anya said. "What about you? You need some dry clothes?"

Stella looked down at her sweater and jacket. They were a bit damp—but not too bad. "I think I'm fine."

Anya held out her arms. "Then you'd better get to school," she said. "I'll finish warming up Rufus and keep a special eye on him during the day."

Stella got to her feet, suddenly anxious about being late. Mrs. Orne hated that. And Stella couldn't risk getting a detention. Not that day.

"Do you think he'll be okay without me?" Stella asked as she put Rufus in Anya's lap. "Because Josie and I are supposed to go to the equine auction this afternoon."

Anya raised an eyebrow. "How come?"

"We want to buy Everest," Stella said.

Anya nodded slowly, absorbing this information.

Stella fidgeted nervously, worrying that Anya would ask a bunch of questions she couldn't answer. Questions like where they were going to keep Everest and how they were going to pay for his food.

"How about if I give you guys a ride?" Anya said finally. "You don't mind if I tag along, do you?"

"No! Thanks!" Relief surged through Stella. She flung herself at Anya and hugged her around the neck. "Thanks, Aunt Anya!"

"You're welcome. I'll pick you guys up after school. Now scoot!"

Stella gave Rufus a get-well kiss and rushed off to school. *Everything is going to work out fine,* she decided.

• 10 •

Stella made it to school just as the bell was ringing. She didn't have time to talk to Josie before class. Stella glanced back at Josie as she slid into her seat.

Josie was slumped forward at her desk. She shook her head slowly, telling Stella that her father had refused to give her the money to buy Everest.

"Okay, people, let's get to work," Mrs. Orne said. She picked up the chalk and moved toward the board.

Stella sighed and faced front. The hour and a half before morning recess stretched on endlessly. With part of her mind, Stella listened to Mrs. Orne explaining long division. At the same time, she was wondering how they could save Everest.

Finally the recess bell rang. Josie came up to Stella's desk. "How much money do you have?" she asked as the girls moved toward the hallway.

Stella had been saving her allowance for Christmas presents. "Twenty dollars," she said.

"I only have six," Josie told her as they moved with their class toward the playground. Her brow was wrinkled with concern.

"How much will we need?" Stella asked.

"I've been thinking about that," Josie said. "Everest isn't that healthy, but I'm not sure that matters considering . . . considering what they want to do with him. I think we need at least a hundred and fifty dollars."

A hundred and fifty dollars! Stella thought, pushing open the door that led outside. It was impossible. She pulled herself up onto the stone wall that surrounded the playground and began to think.

"What's wrong with you two?" Marisa Capra asked as she joined them. Marisa was a pretty girl with heavy dark hair and hazel eyes.

Jared Frye ran up. "You guys want to play dodgeball?" he asked.

Stella shook her head.

"We have to save a pony from the slaughterhouse," Josie explained. "Do you guys have any money?"

"Can you believe people eat pony meat?" Stella put in.

Jared shuddered and shook his head. He put his hand in his pocket, pulled out a handful of change, and began to count it.

Marisa crossed her arms, tipped her head to one side, and studied Josie. "You want to save a pony?" she asked, raising an eyebrow.

"Why not?" Josie snapped.

"It just seems out of character," Marisa said. "I mean, your family ships—what? a few thousand cows to slaughterhouses each year. I wouldn't think the idea would bother you much."

Josie met Marisa's challenging look. "This is different," she said.

"Why?" Marisa asked with some heat. "Just because he has a name? Because he's a *pony* and not a cow?"

"Yes!" Josie shot back.

Stella felt like groaning. She understood what was bothering Marisa, but she didn't think this was the time for a big debate. They needed to concentrate on saving Everest. But Marisa and Josie were *always* ready to argue with each other.

"Ponies are smarter than cows," Josie declared. "And cuter."

"Cows are cute," Stella said. She hadn't meant

to get involved with her friends' argument. The words had just slipped out.

Jared looked up from his counting. "My grandma in Pennsylvania loves cows," he said. "She collects them. Cow clocks, cow salt and pepper shakers, cow cookie jars."

Josie's face was red and she was pursing her lips. "Does your grandmother eat hamburgers?" she demanded.

"Sure," Jared said.

"Then she has no right to judge me and my family," Josie said hotly. She pointed at Marisa and Stella. "And neither do you or you."

"I didn't say anything!" Stella was wounded.

"Don't talk to me about how cute cows are until you become a vegetarian," Josie said. "How do you think all of those nice steaks and hamburgers get to the grocery store?"

"Fine," Marisa said. "I'll never eat meat again. And neither will Stella."

"Let Stella speak for herself!" Josie yelled.

Marisa and Josie were both staring at Stella, challenging her to take a side. Stella opened her mouth and then closed it. Her mind was racing. She didn't know what to say. She'd honestly never thought about giving up meat. It seemed like a big decision to make so quickly.

"I—I'll have to think about it," Stella said. "But

what about Everest? We only have a few minutes of recess left."

The bell rang. Kids started streaming toward the building.

"I have a dollar and twenty-two cents," Jared said quickly. He reached out and poured the change into Stella's hand.

Josie was still glaring at Marisa, breathing heavily through her nose.

Marisa turned to Stella. "I have twenty-seven dollars saved up. My mom is coming to get me after school. I'll get the money from her then."

"Thanks," Stella said. "That will be a big help."

Marisa turned and walked off.

Josie still hadn't moved. "Marisa really has a lot of nerve," she said bitterly.

"Don't be mad." Stella put an arm around Josie's shoulders and steered her toward the building. "She *is* going to lend us twenty-seven dollars. How much money does that make altogether?" she asked, hoping to distract Josie from the argument.

Josie thought about it. "Just over fifty-four dollars," she announced.

The girls were quiet as they made their way down the crowded hallway. Fifty-four dollars wasn't anywhere near what Josie said they needed.

"Maybe it will be enough," Stella said as they turned into the classroom.

"It has to be," Josie said. But she didn't sound very hopeful.

Stella spent the rest of the day in a state of nervous anticipation. She wanted school to last forever. She was dreading the auction, dreading not being able to save Everest.

"I'll see you outside," Marisa told Stella when the dismissal bell rang. Marisa wouldn't look at Josie.

Stella nodded. She waited for Josie to get her books. They walked outside together.

Marisa was standing on the curb next to her mother's fancy truck. She came up to Stella and Josie, holding out a wad of bills.

Stella hung back so that Josie would take the money.

Josie grabbed the bills and dropped her gaze without smiling. She still wasn't ready to forgive Marisa.

"Thanks," Stella said.

"Good luck," Marisa told her. "Call me and tell me what happens."

Josie was counting the money, turning the bills around so they all faced the same way. Her head snapped up. "This is more than twenty-seven dollars," she said in surprise.

Marisa nodded. "My mom put in fifty."

"Wow," Josie said. Then she sullenly added, "Thanks, Marisa."

"Good luck," Marisa repeated.

The school yard was starting to clear out when Anya pulled in. Josie and Stella climbed into her truck. Josie sat next to the window because she got carsick.

The girls were quiet as Anya pulled out of the school yard and headed out of town. "You guys okay?" Anya asked.

"Sure," Stella said.

"Nervous?" Anya asked.

Josie and Stella nodded. The ride to the auction yard was quiet and tense. Stella didn't think they had any hope of winning Everest. Yet she knew they had to try.

The auction yard was a large low building made of unpainted cement blocks and sheet metal. No windows. A cold, businesslike building.

Anya pulled into the mostly empty parking lot. There were half a dozen small horse trailers, including Mr. Harden's. Stella, Josie, and Anya got out and followed an elderly man toward the entrance.

"Look," Josie said, grabbing Stella's arm.

A huge eighteen-wheeler with the words COTTER'S FANCY MEATS painted on the side had just pulled into the lot. Stella watched as it eased to a stop near the entrance. Two men hopped out. The younger one lit a cigarette and leaned up against the huge truck to wait. The other man, who was older, quickly ducked inside the building.

"That's got to be the guy from the slaughter-house," Josie said.

Stella nodded. They went through the door and into the building. Directly in front of them was a large ring surrounded by low bleachers.

They wandered into the ring. From there Stella could see aisles extending off into the distance like spokes on a bike. Steel bars separated the space into holding pens.

"Hello, ladies and gentlemen," came a voice over a loudspeaker. "Please take your seats so we can get started."

People began to wander out of the aisles and find seats around the ring. Stella saw Mr. Harden sitting off to her left. The man from the slaughter-house was seated near the podium.

Behind the podium stood another man. He banged a gavel and spoke into the microphone. "Lot one. A three-year mare and her foal. Bidding starts at twenty dollars. Do I hear twenty dollars?"

A hired hand led the animals into the center of the ring. Stella braced herself, expecting the mare and foal to be sick and sad-looking. She was surprised when the animals actually looked fairly sleek.

The man from the slaughterhouse stood up. "Twenty!" he yelled.

"Oh, no," Stella said. These animals didn't belong at a slaughterhouse!

"Twenty!" The auctioneer pointed at the man from the slaughterhouse. "Do I hear twenty-five?"

The elderly man who had been ahead of them in the parking lot stood up. "Twenty-five!" he yelled.

"Twenty-five!" the auctioneer called. "Do I hear thirty?"

Back and forth the bidding went, quickly running up to over $200. The elderly man finally won the horses for $215.

Stella and Josie exchanged worried looks. "I hope we have enough money," Josie whispered while another group of animals was led out and the bidding began again.

"What are you going to do if someone else is bidding for Everest?" Anya asked the girls.

"Then I'll let him go," Josie told her. "I just want to save him from the slaughterhouse. Okay, Stella?"

"Fine with me," Stella said.

"Lot number three!" the auctioneer yelled. "We have a single brown-and-white pony. Only three years old. No deformities."

Josie grabbed Stella's hand as they watched Everest walk into the ring. He looked worn-out and thin.

"Not much meat on him," the auctioneer said. "We'll start the bidding at ten dollars."

Stella held her breath. Who would possibly want such a sad pony? Her question was answered when the man from the slaughterhouse stood up and yelled, "Ten dollars!"

• 11 •

We have ten!" the auctioneer said, pointing at the man from the slaughterhouse. "Do I hear fifteen? Fifteen?"

Josie hesitated.

Stella held her breath, scanning the crowd. Was anyone else interested in buying Everest? The people in the stands were chatting, making notes, peering into bags. Stella saw one man wave at Anya. Nearly everyone in the county knew Anya. Nobody—except for Mr. Harden—was paying attention to the auction.

"Do I hear fifteen?" the auctioneer asked again.

Josie stood up. "Fifteen!"

For a second, Stella thought the auctioneer

hadn't heard her. But then he pointed at Josie and said, "Fifteen. Do we have twenty?"

"Twenty," said the man from the slaughter-house.

Josie was still on her feet. "Twenty-five!" she said, louder this time.

"Thirty," said the man from the slaughterhouse. Stella shifted nervously.

"Thirty-five!" Josie called out. She kept her eyes forward, her back straight. Stella could tell from the tone of Josie's voice how nervous she was.

"Forty." The man from the slaughterhouse was casual, only half paying attention to the bidding.

"Forty-five!" Josie said.

People in the audience were starting to pay attention now. They whispered and studied Everest curiously—as if wondering why anyone would be interested in such a skinny pony.

Fifty.

Fifty-five.

Sixty.

Sixty-five.

Seventy.

Stella crossed her fingers and willed the man from the slaughterhouse to drop out. *Quit bidding,* she said to herself. *Quit bidding.*

"We have seventy," the auctioneer said. "Do I hear seventy-five?" He looked straight at Josie.

"Seventy-five," Josie said.

"We have seventy-five!" The auctioneer turned his gaze on the man from the slaughterhouse. "Seventy-five! Do I hear eighty. Eighty?"

The man from the slaughterhouse shifted his weight, glanced at Everest. He seemed to be calculating. Then he gave a quick, dismissive shake of his head.

"Sold!" the auctioneer said with a rap of his gavel. "Sold to the lovely young lady with black hair for seventy-five dollars!"

"Yes!" Stella jumped up and gave Josie a hug. They held on to each other, bouncing up and down with excitement.

"You did it!" Stella told Josie as she stepped back.

"Yeah," Josie said, beaming.

"You need to go pay the auctioneer," Anya said.

"Oh—okay!" Josie bounced down the stairs and up to the podium. Stella could see her counting out her money.

She couldn't believe Josie had actually outbid the man from the slaughterhouse. Everest was safe!

Stella felt a little lurch in her stomach when she realized she wasn't sure what was going to happen to Everest now. Mr. Russell might not let Josie keep him.

It doesn't matter, she told herself. Everest was safe—that was the important thing.

Josie came back up the stairs to their seats, waving a slip of white paper. "We have to wait until the auction is over to pick him up," she announced.

"No problem," Anya said. "We can just—" She held up a finger when her cell phone bleeped. She snapped it off her belt and pushed a button. "Hello? Yes, this is Anya Goodwin."

Josie sat down and gave Stella a satisfied grin.

"Do you think your dad will let you keep him?" Stella asked eagerly.

Josie frowned, considering. "Well, I—"

"Lot four!" the auctioneer called out before Josie could respond.

Stella turned toward the ring and saw four horses being led in. Her heart sank. If anything, these animals looked worse off than Everest. Their coats and eyes were dull. They walked with their heads hanging, as if they were only half alive.

Josie stared down at the ring in disbelief.

"Let's start the bidding at twenty dollars," the auctioneer called. "Do I hear twenty?"

"Twenty!" the man from the slaughterhouse called.

Stella felt her happy satisfaction bleed away.

They had saved Everest. That was wonderful. But plenty of ponies and horses were going to leave the auction in that eighteen-wheeler.

"What should we do?" Josie whispered.

"We have twenty!" the auctioneer called. "Do I hear twenty-five? Twenty-five?"

"Bid," Stella said desperately. "We still have some money left."

Josie nodded as if in a dream and rose to her feet. "Twenty-five!" she called.

Anya glanced up in surprise.

"Thirty!" the man from the slaughterhouse said.

"We have thirty!" the auctioneer yelled. "Do I hear thirty-five?"

Josie slowly sank back into her seat. "I don't have thirty-five dollars," she whispered sadly.

A woman in a red sweater on the far end of the ring jumped into the bidding. But before long, she also dropped out. The man from the slaughterhouse won the lot.

"Lot five!" the auctioneer called.

Anya turned off her phone and motioned to Josie and Stella. "Come on, girls," she said. "Let's wait outside. You don't have to sit through this."

Stella and Josie followed Anya out into the cool afternoon air. Stella felt like a coward. Sneaking away wouldn't change what was happening in the ring. The man from the slaughterhouse was going to keep on buying horses whether or not she was there to watch.

Josie was hugging herself and looking miserable.

"So!" Anya said, clearly trying to lighten the mood. "How are you going to get your new pony home?"

"I guess I should call Clem," Josie said dully.

"You can use my phone," Anya said, holding it out. But at that moment, the phone bleeped again. "Just a second," Anya said. "Hello? Yes. Yes—I see. I'll be right there. Umm, maybe twenty minutes? Okay, see you then."

The door opened behind Stella and people began to come out of the building. The auction was over.

Anya clicked off the phone. "Emergency. I've got to get out to the Homesick Ranch. Will you girls be okay on your own?"

Josie and Stella nodded. Anya let Josie use the phone to call Clem. As soon as she knew Clem was on his way, she trotted off toward her truck.

Someone tapped Stella on the back. She spun around and saw Mr. Harden standing right behind her. He was close enough so that Stella could see two black hairs growing out of the tip of his nose.

"You kids want your property?" Mr. Harden grunted.

"Yes, please," Josie said.

"I left him over there." Mr. Harden nodded toward a holding pen. Everest was standing on the outside of the pen, near the split-rail fence.

"Everest!" Josie said. She started toward the pony but Mr. Harden grabbed her arm.

"Get off me," Josie said coldly, shaking loose.

"It's time you fool kids learn to mind your own business," Mr. Harden said.

Stella stood close to Josie, glaring up at Mr. Harden. She was aware of the line of trucks behind her on the driveway, waiting to make a turn onto the busy road in front of the livestock yard. Anya was probably still there somewhere in that line. The trucks made Stella feel safer. Mr. Harden wouldn't hurt them in front of all those people.

"You want to buy a broken-down pony, fine," Mr. Harden said. "No skin off my teeth. Having you here just drove up the price. But anyone asks, you tell them your daddy bought you that pony for a birthday present."

"Why would I do that?" Josie seemed truly baffled.

"Because I told you to," Mr. Harden said.

"He doesn't want his customers to find out!"

Stella exclaimed as she realized the truth. "He's worried tourists won't want to spend money to ride a pony he's going to mistreat—and sell that winter!"

Mr. Harden's face turned tomato red. "I know who you are," he said, waving one fat finger in Stella's face. "Little Stella Sullivan with her letters to the editor and protests. A troublemaker—just like your mama!"

"Come on, Stella." Josie took her friend's arm and started to pull her toward Everest. "Let's go."

Stella shook off Josie. "I think people *should* know how you treat your animals," she told Mr. Harden. "And maybe I'm going to tell them."

Mr. Harden made a nasty sound in his throat and spat at Stella's feet. Stella jumped back. Mr. Harden turned away, pulled out a pistol, and held it up in the air.

BAM!

Stella cowered, holding her hands over her ears. She could see Mr. Harden walking away, the surprised look on Josie's face, Everest pawing at the sky with his front hooves.

"Naaawww!" the pony brayed.

Then he began to run, a panicked bolt away from the loud noise. Stella blinked in surprise. How could the pony have gotten loose? Mr. Harden had tied him to the fence.

Mr. Harden . . . He must have left the lead rope loose.

"Josie, grab him!" Stella called. But she knew it was too late. Everest was rushing straight toward the busy road.

• 12 •

Stella cowered on the side of the road. A red truck threw on its brakes and just missed hitting Everest. The car behind it narrowly missed hitting the truck. Traffic stopped.

"Git hold of that darn pony!" a man yelled out of the window of the red truck.

The pony looked wildly about him. His eyes rolled back in fear. People began to honk their horns.

Stella saw her chance. She darted in front of the red truck, eyes on Everest's loose rope.

"No!" Josie yelled. She ran forward, grabbed Stella, and yanked her back—just as a truck going the other way screeched to a halt.

Stella fell hard onto her bottom.

Clunk! Clunkclunkclunk! Everest's hooves came down on a car roof with a sickening clatter.

Stella and Josie stumbled to their feet. They scrambled back onto the road. Stella looked up to see Everest galloping through an open lot bordering the road.

"Now what?" Josie asked.

Stella was shaking. She kept seeing an image of the truck passing inches in front of her nose, and hearing the sound of Mr. Harden's pistol firing. "I—I don't know," she admitted.

The trucks coming out of the parking lot began to snake toward the road again. A moment later, Anya's familiar green truck pulled up next to them. Anya spoke to them through her open window. "Girls, what happened? Are you okay?"

"Everest got away," Stella said.

"Climb in," Anya said. "Let's see if we can catch him."

The girls carefully checked traffic. Then they ran around the truck and climbed in. Anya drove up to the road and turned left. She pulled over to the shoulder of the road and drove slowly.

Stella and Josie sat sideways on the seat, anxiously scanning the empty lot. Brown scrubby grass. No trees. No buildings. No place for Everest to hide. But Stella couldn't see him.

"Where did he go?" Anya wondered.

"I wish I had a horse," Josie muttered, her voice tight with tension. "We don't know if Everest is going to stay near the road. He could be heading for the woods behind that empty lot. He could have doubled back toward the livestock yard."

Stella could feel her friend's panic. She knew just how she felt. Stella had felt the same way when Rufus had been lost during a forest fire that summer.

Then Stella saw something out of the corner of her eye. "What was that?" she asked.

"What? Where?" Anya asked.

"Up ahead," Stella said. "See that empty store? I thought I saw a flash of brown behind it."

The store was a rambling, low-slung wooden structure. The windows were boarded up with big pieces of plywood. Anya pulled into the sprawling, vacant parking lot.

Josie pushed open the door and jumped out as soon as the truck slowed to a stop. She ran around the side of the building.

Stella hurried after her, hearing the crunch of their boots on the gravel. She turned the corner and saw Everest facing her. Josie had her arms wrapped around his neck, her face buried in his fur.

Anya came up behind Stella. "Great," she said.

Stella nodded, her heart aching with happiness. Everything was going to be all right.

Josie looked up at them, her eyes bright with tears. "Anya," she said with a sniffle, "Everest's legs are all scratched up. Can you look at them?"

Anya stepped forward, and Stella saw she had her horse bag in one hand. While Stella and Josie soothed the pony, Anya cleaned the cuts. She wrapped a bandage around Everest's front right leg. His other legs didn't need bandaging.

When they were finished, Anya once again headed out on her emergency. Josie and Stella led Everest across the frozen grass back toward the stockyard—maybe a quarter of a mile away.

Everest was peaceful now, passively clomping along behind them. Josie was smiling as if she had gotten straight A's on her report card.

Clem's truck with the Russells' horse trailer hitched behind was the only vehicle in the stockyard. Clem dropped out of the truck when he saw them coming. "Where have you been?" he demanded. "I have better things to do than wait for you."

"I know," Josie said patiently. "Everest got away from me."

Clem frowned and turned to study Everest. "Guess he's feeling better, then, huh?"

Josie nodded. "He's spirited!"

Stella stayed out of the way while Clem and Josie gently loaded the pony into the trailer. They didn't talk—they didn't have to. They'd worked together all of their lives, and their actions fit neatly together.

"You riding back with us?" Josie asked Stella.

"Sure," Stella said. "I have to see Everest in his new home."

"Home?" Clem snorted and shook his head. "Don't know what Dad is going say about us taking in a scrawny pony."

The three of them were quiet as they rode back to the Russells'. Clem went off somewhere while Josie and Stella unloaded Everest. Soon the pony was in his cozy stall, munching on some best-quality hay.

Josie and Stella stood at the end of his stall, still amazed to see him there. Enjoying their victory.

Stella heard footsteps on the concrete aisle. She turned, expecting to see Clem. But it was Mr. Russell coming toward them. He wasn't smiling. His hands were stuffed down into his pockets. Stella felt Josie tense up.

Mr. Russell stopped behind them. He stood staring in at the pony. Mr. Russell was breathing heavily.

Stella couldn't breathe at all. She felt like slinking away. She knew Mr. Russell didn't approve of her. He thought she was a troublemaker—just like Mr. Harden did.

But Stella couldn't leave Josie to face her father alone. What if Mr. Russell said Everest had to go? Everest would be okay. They'd find another home for the pony, Stella knew. But what about Josie? She would be heartbroken.

"Hi, Daddy," Josie said fearfully.

"Hay isn't free, you know," Mr. Russell said gruffly.

"I know," Josie said, her eyes lowered.

Stella listened as Mr. Russell breathed in and out. "His feed is coming out of your allowance," he said.

Josie's head snapped up, and a smile crept over her face. "Ah—sure!" she said. "No problem."

"Give him some oats," Mr. Russell said gruffly. "Fatten him up. Animals in my barn don't look like that."

"Okay, Daddy!" Josie said joyfully.

He was already moving down the aisle, too busy to waste any more time on them.

" 'Bye, Mr. Russell!" Stella said.

"Stella," he said without turning around.

Josie threw her arms around Stella and they shared a hug. When Stella looked up, she saw Everest watching them curiously. She wondered if he understood that he had just been granted a long and happy life.

*　　*　　*

The next afternoon Stella's family gathered around the big living room table for Thanksgiving dinner. The table was full of platters of steaming food. Stella's father, Jack, always went all out on holidays.

Anya was there. So were Boris and Chewy. They were out in the yard, having their own Thanksgiving celebration with Rufus.

Bud was sitting next to Stella. She thought he looked strange without his baseball cap and uniform. He was wearing a nice shirt and a tie.

Everyone was a little dressed up. Anya was wearing slacks—not jeans—and a blue sweater Stella had never seen before. Stella had on her party dress, which had gotten a little tight across the shoulders since the last time she had worn it. She felt itchy.

"Let's give thanks," Norma said as she slid into her seat. Everyone joined hands.

Stella's family had a tradition. Each year on Thanksgiving, everyone around the table said what they were thankful for.

"I'll begin," Norma said solemnly. "I'm thankful for my wonderful family. And I'm thankful to live in such beautiful country surrounded by nature."

Jack squeezed Norma's hand. "I'm thankful for my family, too. And I'm thankful I don't have to do all these dishes."

Stella groaned along with the others. Then she turned to Cora, who was next.

Cora screwed up her face, thinking. "Um, I'm thankful for horses and cute boys and sleeping late on Saturday. Oh, and Dad's pecan pie."

Jack gave Cora a wink.

Papa Pete, sitting at the head of the table, was next. "I'm thankful for my health," he said gruffly.

Now, Anya. "I'm thankful for my work," she said with a quiet smile.

Everyone turned to look at Bud. His cheeks were pink and he had slid down in his seat. He kept his eyes glued to his empty plate. "Um . . . ," he whispered. "I'm thankful that Jane is recovering." He glanced at Stella.

"Oh—," Stella said. "I'm thankful Everest found a good home. . . . And I'm thankful for the animal clinic and Aunt Anya. And Mom and Dad and Cora. Um, and Papa Pete. And Rufus!"

Everyone was smiling and laughing as they dropped hands and began passing the food. Stella helped herself to vegetables, stuffing, cranberry sauce, mashed potatoes, and a piece of Bud's homemade bread.

Then Bud held out a huge platter. "Would you like some turkey?" he asked Stella.

"Sure, thanks." Stella picked up the serving fork. She started to help herself.

Stella hesitated as Marisa's and Josie's argument came flooding back into her mind.

Maybe Marisa was right. Maybe eating beef or turkey wasn't any different from eating pony. Who cared that ponies were smarter and cuter?

Turkeys are stupid, but they can feel pain, Stella told herself. And fear. They probably enjoyed life. Killing them just so she could have dinner was wrong! It was cruel!

Or was it?

Stella looked around at her family. Everyone had turkey on their plates. Even Anya, who spent her life trying to save animals' lives. Even Norma, who loved wildlife.

People aren't bunnies, Stella told herself. *We evolved eating meat.* Maybe asking people to give up meat was just as silly as expecting wolves to stop killing elk. Maybe eating meat was just human nature.

"Stella?" Bud said quietly.

"Oh." Stella giggled. Poor Bud had been holding out the platter the entire time she had been debating with herself.

Stella put a small piece of turkey on her plate and pushed it to one side.

No way Stella could ever eat pony or horse. From now on, as long as she lived, ponies would remind her of Josie and how much she loved Everest.

But turkey . . .

Stella had never known anyone who loved a turkey.

At least, not yet.

WHY ISN'T STELLA
A VEGETARIAN?

In this story, Stella's friend Marisa decides to stop eating meat. Marisa pressures Stella to become a **vegetarian,** too. A vegetarian is a person who cuts meat, poultry, and fish out of his or her diet. Stella eventually decides eating turkey and other types of meat is okay—even though she definitely does not want to eat certain animals, like ponies.

Were you surprised by Stella's decision? Did you expect a person who loves animals as much as Stella does to also hate the idea of eating anything with eyes (including potatoes)?

People choose their diets for many different reasons. Some are influenced by religious beliefs, others by where they live. Most everyone has a tendency to love the foods they've been brought up eating. Stella makes her decision because the people she loves and respects most—Anya and her own parents—are meat eaters.

What decision is right for you? To help you decide, here are some of the reasons people decide not to eat meat, as well as some arguments on the other side. Read on!

Arguments for becoming a vegetarian

- Eating animals that may have emotions and intelligence strikes some people as **morally wrong.** They say animals have as much right to a long and healthy life as humans do.
- By eating only vegetables and grains, you're saying no to **cruelty to animals.** Some animals raised for food—especially chickens and calves raised for veal—live their entire lives in small, cramped cages.
- Meat can be **unhealthy.** Too much red meat like beef or lamb can clog up your arteries and hurt your heart. Some ranchers feed their livestock hormones or antibiotics. These feed additives may make some people sick.
- Raising livestock is hard on the **environment.** Cattle use up huge amounts of limited resources like water and land. Herds of cattle can

damage topsoil which is essential to keeping pastures fertile and streams clean. Cattle emit methane, carbon dioxide, and nitrous oxide when they fart. These emissions may be contributing to a dangerous warming of the earth's atmosphere.

- Two-thirds of the grain grown in the United States go to feed cattle and other livestock. Many people feel that grain should go to feed **hungry people** instead.
- Some people simply don't like the **taste of meat**.

Arguments for eating meat

- The killing of animals for food is the **natural order** of things. Asking humans to give up meat is just as silly as expecting lions or sharks to go veggie.
- A **balanced diet is a key to good health**— especially for growing kids. Some vitamins that are easy to get from meat are difficult to obtain from fruits and vegetables.
- **Farm animals have it good** compared to their wild counterparts. Most ranchers make sure their animals are never hungry, thirsty, or stressed. By contrast, animals in the wild often die slow and

painful deaths from disease, starvation, or because a predator turns them into dinner.

- **Humans are omnivores**—animals that evolved eating a wide variety of foods. Our bodies naturally crave fruits, vegetables, grains, dairy products, *and* meat.
- Meat, poultry, and fish **taste good** to many people.
- Focusing on your diet too much could lead to an **unhealthy attitude** toward food.

How many vegetarians are there?

Both sides have some strong arguments. But most people in the United States do eat meat. Studies show that only one to five percent of Americans are strict vegetarians who never eat meat, poultry, or fish. That number has stayed about the same for a decade or so.

However, vegetarians have changed what many Americans eat. Compared to a decade ago, many more Americans are now trying to eat veggie dinners two or three nights a week. Most of these people hope cutting some meat out of their diets will make them healthier.

Vegetarians have also influenced the way some animals are raised. Farms raising free-range chickens popped up after people complained that chickens raised in coops were unhealthy. Many people have given up veal because animal rights protests have publicized how the animals are kept in small stalls.

People seem to feel better about eating meat when they know the animals didn't suffer during their lives or when they were slaughtered.

What do you think? Emily Costello, the author of the *Animal Emergency* series, would like to hear your opinion. Send her an e-mail at **emily@enarch-ma.com** or write to her care of HarperCollins Children's Books.